The Stone Beach

KIM CHATEL

More books by Kim Chatel

Rainbow Sheep
A Talent For Quiet
Burgher and the Woebegone
Horse Camp
Clip-clop, Tippity-tap: Frech Vocabulary
on the Farm
Once, Twice Thrice

For Genevieve, who asks the big questions.
And for Casey, of course.

Chapter One

Caroline's friends liked electronic dance music that made her head hurt, but she thought the sweetest music in the world rumbled out of Casey's chest when he purred. Though he was getting old, Casey's purr was strong and sweet. She fell asleep every night with her finger twined in his thick, orange fur, feeling the vibrations of his music tingling up through her fingers, letting sleep creep up on her.

What will I do when he's gone?

No, she pushed those thoughts away. That wasn't the way to fall asleep. She let her hand run down Casey's back, feeling the sharp bones under his skin. His fox-like tail swished under her chin, and Caroline held it there, cuddling it like a favorite bear. Eventually, the purring and the warm weight of the cat comforted her, and she slept.

The next morning, Caroline's mother gave Casey his first shot. The vet had shown them both how to do it the day before, but Caroline was afraid to hurt Casey. She understood he needed his medicine, but she hated to see the needle.

Mom saw her face and smiled. "You know it doesn't hurt him. Look, he barely feels it." She pinched the skin behind Casey's shoulder and stuck in the needle.

"You're so brave!" Caroline said to Casey and gave him a shrimp treat. Once, the shrimp bites had been a rare treat, but Casey was so skinny now, he could eat as many as he wanted. So Caroline snuck him another. Long auburn hair hid her face. Tears and words stuck in her throat. Mom put an arm around her and waited for Caroline to speak.

She had so many thoughts and worries she didn't know how to put into words. But she would try. She took a deep breath.

"What if, one morning, Casey doesn't wake up?"

Mom kissed the top of her head and held her close. Caroline thought she was too old for hugs, but she didn't pull away.

"It might happen," Mom said. "I can't promise otherwise. So we have to love him as much as we can while he's still here with us, right?"

Caroline nodded and petted Casey as he ate his

treats. Later she would brush him in the sunshine and make a bed for him out of his favorite blankets.

Casey was older than she was. At sixteen, he was old for a cat. Last spring, Mom had noticed he'd lost weight, and they'd taken him to see the veterinarian. Casey stayed in the hospital for three days while they did tests and fed him special medicines through a tube in his front leg. Caroline visited him every day after school. Careful not to irritate the shunt, she'd take him out of his cage to hold him in her lap while she sang his favorite "Soft Kitty" song. Each day, when she put him back in the cage, his eyes begged her not to abandon him again and her heart broke a little more.

"He can go home now," Dr. Kowolsky said on the fourth day. "I can't do much more for him here."

Caroline cuddled Casey close to her chest. He purred a deep rumble, but the pads of his feet were damp with worried sweat.

"Thank God," she said. "I couldn't bear to put him back in that cage again."

Dr. Kowolsky smiled. "You take good care of him, Caroline. He's a lucky cat. As long as you give him his medicine every day, he'll be all right."

Caroline knew the doctor meant all right for an old cat, and that was months ago. Casey had shrunk since then. His skin hung down as if he wore another cat's fur coat. He limped and meowed for water all the time. Sometimes he didn't know what he wanted, but wandered aimlessly, crying for some treat he couldn't name.

Now, on a bright September morning, Caroline sat outside in the sun with a lump of Casey's orange fur clutched in her hand. After his brushing, he'd fallen sleep in the shade. Caroline let the fur fly away on the wind.

He shouldn't be losing so much fur. Even the warm weather couldn't account for the clumps of fur that came off on her brush.

Clouds dotted the blue sky and the wind would bring more. Today was the last day of summer vacation, and Caroline was glad to see it go. Usually, she was bummed when back-to-school came around. Fall meant back to homework, boring classes and rushed mornings, but this year she was eager to be among her friends again. Last spring, her family had moved to this old farmhouse in the country. They hadn't changed school districts, but they lived in the sticks now. Before the move, Brenda, her best friend, had lived just down the street. They'd seen each other every day, slept over at each other's houses most nights. She still saw Brenda and the others, but only when Mom could drive her across town. Without her usual friends, summer had dragged on like one endless sunny day with nothing to do but stare at the green trees.

Yes, school would be a welcome change. Even homework sounded like fun.

Her father came to sit on the lawn beside her with his coffee mug in one hand. Mom and Dad loved the farm. They gardened and took long walks. Dad had converted the old barn into an office and workroom, so he no longer had to commute to the city.

"What are your plans for the last day of summer," he asked.

"I wanted to visit Brenda, but she's not home."

"I guess you'll be glad to get back to school."

Caroline said nothing. She didn't want to hurt her father's feelings, but she'd be glad to get away from the farm. Caroline knew she should be grateful for the extra time they now spent together as a family, and she was. It was all the rest of the time, when she had nothing to do and no one to see that bothered her. She thought she might implode from sheer boredom before the end of this last summer day.

"I miss my friends, that's all."

"I know this summer has been a disappointment," he said. "I wanted you to love this place as much as I do. I've got plans to build a new gazebo. You could help out. I could even show you how to use my power tools."

Caroline smiled and shook her head.

"Not really your thing, I guess," he said. "Well, why don't you make friends with the girl at the next homestead. What's her name?"

Caroline wrinkled her nose like she'd smelled something bad.

"You mean Aimee Jones?"

"Yeah. Their place is only a half-mile down the road."

"Aimee Jones doesn't have any friends, Dad. And she likes it that way."

"Oh, I doubt that. Everybody needs friends."

"You don't understand. If you knew her, you wouldn't want us to be friends."

"Why not? She's not into drugs, is she?"

"No. Nothing like that. But she's weird. She sits by herself at recess reading, ignoring everyone around her. And she doesn't like to be disturbed. Once, she took a basketball which had bounced on her book and threw it over the fence into the street. The boy who owned it called Aimee some terrible names."

"Did she get mad?"

"I guess. It's hard to tell. Aimee never raises her voice. But she punched the guy in the stomach hard enough wind him."

"Ouch," Dad said. "Well, sometimes you find friends in unlikely places. Think of it as a community service."

"I'd rather pick up garbage along the highway," Caroline mumbled. Dad laughed and ruffled her hair.

"You could sit here and be bored instead."

He went back to his office and Caroline let herself out the back garden gate, ignoring the hummingbirds on the flowering bushes and the squirrels chattering in the trees overhead.

She wouldn't visit Aimee Jones. That girl was scary. Her hair, dyed blue-black, was always a mess, as if she'd styled it that way. She wore black peasant dresses and combat boots along with enough silver jewelry and piercings to make a pirate envious. If Brenda and her crowd saw Caroline with Aimee, first they'd laugh, and then they'd never speak to her again. No, she couldn't be friends with Aimee. It was better to have no friends than the wrong friends.

She took the wooded path to the river. Mom didn't want her to play near the water, but there was so little to do. She sat on a large rock and watched the current zip past, wondering what Brenda was doing today? Had she found a new best friend? Did she still play with Jimmy? Brenda had said she was too old to play with boys, but Caroline suspected she still joined in for soccer-baseball with Jimmy and his brothers. Caroline would, if she had the chance.

She picked up a stone and tossed it into the river. "Hey! Watch it!"

Caroline looked up and froze. Aimee crouched in the water with a small net in her hand. Her clothes were so dirty she blended in with the scenery. Caroline hadn't even seen her. Aimee glared at Caroline, before settling back on her ankles to gaze at the water.

After a tense moment, Caroline realized Aimee would not jump up and beat her into a pulp. When she could breathe again, Caroline wanted to know what Aimee was doing, but didn't dare disturb her. Aimee was unpredictable. And crazy. Caroline should just go home. But she really wanted to know what Aimee was staring at.

Aimee continued to crouch in the rushing water, almost as still as one of the river stones. Curiosity won out, and Caroline clambered over the bank to peer over Aimee's shoulder. There were no fish in the water. Nothing that she could see except for the gray and black stones that lined this part of the river.

"You can't see from there, stupid," Aimee said. "Get in the water."

Caroline didn't worry about being called stupid. Aimee never spoke without using some insult or swear word. Luckily, she didn't speak much.

Caroline couldn't see any other shoes on the shore, but she took hers off and stepped into the shockingly cold water. The rocks were slippery, and she lost her footing. A strong arm shot out and grabbed her wrist.

"You'll scare them away, jerk wad."

"Sorry. I've never walked in the river before."

"No kidding," Aimee said sarcastically. "You should wear an old pair of runners, or you'll slip and kill yourself."

Caroline looked down at Aimee's bare feet.

Aimee shrugged. "I've been river-walking forever. Besides, I like to feel the rocks and sand under my feet."

Caroline couldn't understand what was so great about rocks and sand. They were rough-edged and pointy. She gritted her teeth and tried to ignore the pain in her feet. She nearly slipped again and hung onto the other girl. Aimee didn't shrug her off.

They stood quietly for a few minutes. Aimee stared at a large underwater rock.

"What are you waiting for?" Caroline asked.

"Crawfish. Under that big rock."

Crawfish? Don't they have pinchers? She shifted her feet, and a cloud of sand stirred up from the bottom, blocking the rock from their view.

"Idiot!" Aimee hissed. "It probably escaped in that mess."

Caroline waited for Aimee to turn on her, to punch her in the face or give a good elbow to the gut, but nothing happened. Instead, she stood up and stretched.

"Come on. I'll show you something." She walked off down the river. Caroline stumbled along behind. She cut her feet on the jagged rocks and slipped twice, soaking herself, but Aimee didn't stop. Caroline rested for a moment on a large rock in the middle of the stream. The current was strong here. It swirled around her ankles like a racetrack. Up ahead, Aimee walked the river with ease. Caroline never imagined that she'd be envious of Aimee Jones. She wondered what Brenda would think if she saw her now. She wanted to turn back. Her mother would have a fit if she knew Caroline was in the river. She glanced at the shore, judging the current. It looked stronger than the current up ahead, but she wanted to get out of the water now.

"Come on," Aimee said impatiently. "It gets easier just around the bend."

Caroline sighed and stumbled forward again, trying to ignore the smirk on Aimee's face. She slipped on a slimy stone, stubbed her toe and scraped her ankle. One painful step after another until Caroline finally caught up.

"Look." Aimee pointed.

As they turned the bend, the sun broke through the thin clouds. Caroline took another step forward to see around the trees, and heaven opened up in front of her. At least it was what Caroline imagined how heaven would look. The river widened and deepened. The water was still as glass, and yet the current tugged at her ankles. Cicadas buzzed in the trees. A family of ducks floated in the shade beneath the weeping willows to her left. All this beauty was eclipsed by the stone beach—a small sandbar stretching along the right bank, covered in pink stones sparkling in the sunlight.

Caroline had grown up in a development with sidewalks, streetlights and a little park at the end of the cul-de-sac. This sweep of the river was the most beautiful place she'd ever seen.

"It's deep enough to swim," Aimee said as she walked forward a couple of steps. The water rose to her thighs. Caroline laughed and Aimee grinned back at her before diving, fully clothed, into the water.

Why not? Caroline's shorts and T-shirt were soaked anyway. She dove into the water after Aimee and was amazed at the soft riverbed. Instead of the sharp rocks she had expected, she dug her toes into soft sand. Then she fell back in the water again and raised her feet high in the air, letting sand and water splash over her.

They splashed around for a few minutes, and then Aimee crept up on the ducks. They circled her for a moment before swimming away in a line, as if expecting Aimee to follow.

"That's amazing," Caroline said. "Why don't they fly away?"

"She's the mother," Aimee said, pointing to the largest duck. "I've been coming here so long, she thinks I'm one of her ducklings."

Caroline realized then what Aimee had done. She'd brought Caroline to her quiet place, her special hideout where she came to get away from everyone. Caroline had a quiet place at her old house, an almost impenetrable thicket of bushes in the park at the end of the block. With Brenda, she'd found a break in the branches big enough for them to crawl through. The center of the thicket had been cleared out, probably by older kids, now long gone. It made a great fort, and they'd sworn to each other they'd keep it a secret.

Once, when her parents were on her case about homework and chores, Caroline had stayed in the thicket until long after dark. Her parents had been frantic, but the quiet place had done its job, and she'd been able to go home and deal with them.

This river was Aimee's thicket, and Caroline felt embarrassed to be sharing it with her. Then Aimee splashed her and called her a nasty name. Caroline laughed and ducked under the water, grabbing at Aimee's leg. She forgot her shyness with the strange girl—forgot that she wasn't supposed to make friends with the school freak—and they played in the water all afternoon.

Finally worn out, the girls took turns floating on their backs. Aimee held the record time at seventy-six seconds.

"Oh look," she said, as Caroline floated on her back, trying to break the record. "A leech."

"A what?" She felt something brush past her leg and screamed. She scrambled toward shore and crawled hands over feet onto the beach of pink rocks, then flopped down and frantically slapped at her legs.

Still in the water, Aimee laughed so hard, she nearly went under. Caroline glared at her, then inspected her legs. There were no bloodsuckers.

"That's not funny!"

Aimee lay down on the rocks beside her, laughing. "You should have seen your face!"

Caroline's stomach was jittery from the fright, but she laughed too. Then, exhausted, they lay on the rocks and enjoyed the warm sun.

"Why are they pink," Caroline asked, "the rocks, I mean." As far down the river as she could see, the pink rocks shone like jewels.

Aimee threw an arm over her eyes to shade them from the sun. "I dunno. Maybe they're enchanted fairy treasure."

"Yeah, right." Caroline laughed.

Aimee smiled, but for a moment, Caroline thought she actually blushed.

"I gotta get home." Aimee stood and turned toward the forest without a goodbye.

"See you at school tomorrow," Caroline called after her.

"Yeah, whatever."

What did I do? Sometime during the afternoon, Caroline had forgotten the solitary, ill-mannered Aimee and her reappearance was a surprise.

Caroline sat in the sun until her clothes dried. She picked up pink stones, one by one. Black lines veined through them and they sparkled with bits of quartz. Each was different and yet similar, as if they had all been crushed from one giant stone.

She thought about Aimee's sudden departure and felt like she'd tamed a wild creature for the afternoon. But as soon as it remembered its wildness, it had run away. Had she said something to upset Aimee? They'd been talking about the pink stones, and then

Aimee had said that weird thing about fairies and taken off. Could she really believe in fairies? Or was she embarrassed to talk about something so girlie?

Very strange.

Brenda would never believe she'd spent the afternoon with crazy Aimee Jones, but Caroline wasn't exactly going to broadcast it to her friends anyway. She put one of the pink stones in the pocket of her cutoff jeans to prove to herself at least it had really happened.

Chapter Two

Caroline was late for the bus. "Don't forget to give Casey his medicine," she called to Mom as she hurried out the door. She wanted to say goodbye to him, but didn't have time. Every day could be his last, so she tried to cuddle him a bit each morning. Missing him left her grumpy.

Great way to start the new school year, she thought as she ran toward the bus stop. The road was unpaved, and she stumbled on a rock, twisting her ankle painfully.

One more reason to hate this farm.

The bus waited for her on the corner. She jumped inside and thanked the driver as they rumbled down the road.

In the front seat, Aimee already had her nose stuck in a book.

"Hey," Caroline said, but Aimee didn't respond.

Two eighth-grade girls called to Caroline from the back of the bus. Better than sitting alone. She looked at Aimee over her shoulder as she made her way down the aisle. Aimee didn't look up from her book. Soon, the girls were regaling her with stories about their fantastic summers. Caroline forgot her hectic morning and Aimee's slight.

The first day of school was always a rush of excitement. Brenda grabbed her in a big hug as soon as she got off the bus.

"You cut your hair!" Caroline said. "You look so different." Brenda had cut her dark hair in a bob. She also filled out her sweater better than Caroline remembered, and was she wearing eye-shadow?

"And you look exactly the same," Brenda said. "I've got Peterson for home-room."

"Eeww!" Caroline smiled and the two girls headed, arm-in-arm, into the courtyard. They'd heard stories about Mr. Peterson. He threw things when he was mad, which was most of the time, but the worst thing was his smell, like he never washed. "Better add nose-plugs to your list of school supplies."

Brenda laughed while she looked over her shoulder to be sure no teachers had heard them.

"I've got Miss Besner," Caroline said.

"Oh, lucky you. My brother had her. Sit in the

back of the class. Besner is so old; she can't see that far. She'll never call on you."

"Thanks for the tip." Caroline wanted to hear all about Brenda's summer, but Brenda wasn't listening anymore. Jimmy Douglas had caught her attention. He came toward them from the end of the hall. Caroline barely recognized him. He'd grown at least two inches during the summer.

"Hey." Jimmy's hair was blonder than Caroline remembered, but he was still the same shy boy they'd picked on since kindergarten.

"Hey," Brenda said.

An awkward silence followed this greeting. Caroline looked from her best friend to the boy and a horrible idea started to form in her head.

"Hey, Jimmy," she said, and he looked at her for the first time.

"Oh, hi Caroline. Had a good summer?"

"Great, you?"

"Yeah, I've got to get to class."

Caroline grinned at him as he walked away. She grabbed Brenda by the arm and dragged her into the corner of the courtyard.

"What's going on?" she demanded. Brenda blushed.

"Nothing. What do you mean?"

"I mean, it looks like you two played more than soccer-baseball this summer."

"Oh Caroline, don't be gross."

Brenda's disgust was not convincing. A boy they'd known since kindergarten shouldn't make her blush. At the start of middle school, they'd both decided the only boys worth noticing were those who came from elementary schools other than their own. The boys they'd known all their lives were babies, while the new boys seemed taller and cuter.

"One summer away, and you go all crazy on me." Caroline's tone was harsher than she'd meant, and Brenda glared at her.

"You're crazy. Jimmy's a friend. I had to have some friends this summer, didn't I? It's not like you made a great effort to see me."

"That's not fair! Just because your mother works doesn't mean you couldn't come and see me!"

"What, and play Old Macdonald with you on the farm?"

"Hey!"

Caroline's retort was cut off by the bell for homeroom. Brenda and Caroline glared at each other and stomped off in opposite directions for class.

Caroline fumed about Brenda throughout the principal's welcome speech over the speaker. Did Brenda think she was stupid? She'd seen the way Jimmy had looked at her, and worse, she'd seen the way Brenda had looked at Jimmy. And what was with the Old Macdonald? Could she get any meaner? Caroline never complained about Brenda's house, even though it was so messy and dirty, she sometimes didn't want to use the bathroom.

What was with Brenda anyway?

By the time old Miss Besner handed out the new ecology text books and told them to read the opening chapter, Caroline's temper had cooled and she could see things through her friend's eyes. Brenda was obviously embarrassed. She got that. After all, Jimmy wasn't one of the cool guys. He never went to any of the dances, which was probably a good thing, because none of the girls would dance with him anyway. Except Brenda, now. Or maybe she wouldn't. Maybe she liked Jimmy but would do nothing about it because she worried about what her friends would say.

Caroline remembered her afternoon with Aimee. She took her pink stone out of her pocket. Under the fluorescent lights, it didn't shine, but it was still beautiful. What would Brenda think about her friendship with Aimee? If it could be called a friendship.

"If you're finished reading, Caroline," Miss Besner said , "you can give us a summary of the chapter."

So much for Besner's poor eyesight.

Caroline mumbled something about not having finished. She tucked the stone back in her pocket and tried to concentrate on ecology.

At recess, Caroline apologized to Brenda.

"I'm sorry I called you crazy. I guess I'm just jealous, because I missed all the fun this summer."

"Yeah, I'm sorry too. I didn't mean to make fun of your house."

"It's okay. It is pretty boring there. I'm glad to be back at school, even if Besner already has it in for me."

"Did I say she was blind?" Brenda laughed. "I meant deaf. Make sure you yell when you speak to her."

Caroline grinned. Brenda was still the practical joker.

"Yeah, that'll go over really well. Hey Besner, you can take your ecology and stuff it!"

The girls nearly fainted with laughter.

"Yeah, well, at least she only teaches about compost," Brenda said. "Peterson smells like compost. For once, I was glad this school doesn't have air conditioning. We had all the windows open instead, and I still thought I would gag."

"I see you guys are already into teacher bashing," said Heather as she walked up to them with a group of girls.

"It's tradition." Caroline smiled, before rushing

in to give each of her friends a hug. They were all excited about their summers, their new classes and the few new boys to the school. Cindy had been selected for Olympic soccer camp. Andrea had spent the summer at her Grandmother's and met an amazing boy. They still wrote to each other. Meg worked for her brother's landscaping company and earned enough to buy a new iPhone. Brenda didn't mention Jimmy, and Caroline didn't have anything exciting to tell. Her summer had been a dud, but she wouldn't let her friends know how lonely she'd been.

She saw Aimee reading on a bench in the corner of the courtyard. Caroline wondered how she could read so much. It seemed unnatural somehow. She waited for Aimee to look up so that she could say hello, but even the noisy laughter of the girls couldn't drag Aimee's attention away.

The bell rang. Aimee stood and headed to class, without looking away from her book. Caroline fell in beside her. Brenda and the other girls walked into the school without even noticing that Caroline had left the group.

"Hey," she said. "What are you reading?"

Aimee glanced at her and shook her head before turning into her classroom.

What's with her? Caroline watched Aimee leave,

but Heather was already calling her to hurry up for math class.

"I don't want to get stuck sitting beside someone really gross."

"Sure," Caroline said, trying not to feel snubbed by the biggest loser in the school.

༄

Because they lived the farthest from school, Aimee and Caroline were the last students off the bus in the afternoons. Aimee sat in the front seat. Caroline had been in the back until her friends left. Now she worked her way to the front.

"What's with the attitude at school?" she asked. Aimee didn't even look up from her book.

"We're not friends."

"What?"

Aimee tucked the book in her backpack as the bus slowed to a stop.

"Because we spent an afternoon together, doesn't make us friends. I don't hang around with your kind." Aimee flung her backpack over her shoulder and stalked off the bus.

Caroline was stunned.

Your kind? What did that mean? The not crazy kind? The kind that didn't punch people?

"You getting off?"

Caroline looked up. She was alone on the bus and the driver was smirking at her.

Maybe I'm the crazy one. Maybe I imagined the whole thing.

At home, she rifled through the cupboard searching for a snack before starting her homework. She was actually looking forward to studying. It was better than wandering around the farm, better than worrying if she was going to run into crazy Aimee Jones. She might even improve her grades this year out of sheer boredom.

Her mother burst into the kitchen.

"Oh good, you're home. Grab your jacket we're going to the vet."

Caroline's heart sank.

Casey!

"What's the matter?" she asked, afraid to know.

"I don't know. Maybe nothing. Let's go."

Caroline held Casey during the ride to the vet. He didn't purr. He didn't fuss. The car usually agitated him, but he lay quietly in her lap. His eyes were open, but droopy. She petted him and kissed his head. She never tired of his smell—like Christmas, warm and crisp all at once.

"It's going to be okay," she whispered in his ear. Mom looked over at her, and Caroline could see the worry on her face.

The vet saw them right away, despite the crowded waiting room. That was never a good sign.

Dr. Kowolsky had been treating Casey since he was a kitten and knew immediately something was wrong.

"He's dehydrated," she said. "The technician is going to take some blood and give him fluids right away, and then I'll be back to examine him more thoroughly."

Caroline nodded.

Dr. Kowolsky always spoke directly to Caroline and not her mother. She knew Casey was her cat, and she didn't treat her like a kid.

The technician had no trouble getting the needle into Casey. Caroline remembered once, when he was younger, Casey had scratched a technician so badly, the woman had needed tending by the doctor. Those were his young and feisty days. Now, he lay listlessly on the steel table and let the tech stick him with whatever she wanted.

Caroline could feel tears welling in her eyes. What if Dr. Kowolsky said they had to put Casey to sleep? Caroline knew the day was coming, but what if it was today? Her worst fear was she wouldn't be brave enough to stay with Casey when they gave him the last needle. She was sure she'd chicken out, no matter how much he needed her.

This thought, more than any other, made her sick to her stomach.

Casey slept in her arms while they waited for the blood test results. Caroline put her head on his back, glad to feel the gentle rise and fall of his breathing.

Finally, the doctor returned. She gave nothing away with her stern expression and Caroline tried to prepare herself for the worst, but really, there was no way to prepare, was there?

"Casey's had a diabetic seizure," she said.

"But I gave him his insulin today," Mom said.

"It's not that. He's actually had too much insulin."

"I don't understand?" Caroline felt panic about to overwhelm her. How could he get too much insulin? They followed the doctor's instructions exactly.

"His diabetes is unstable," Dr. Kowolsky said. "Without a blood test everyday it's hard to gauge how much insulin he really needs."

She prepared a needle and stuck it into the skin behind his shoulder.

"That's a kind of sugar water. It should perk him up a bit. Don't look so worried, Caroline," she smiled. "He's going to be fine. Now let's get a weight on him."

Casey woke up enough to fuss about being put on the scales.

"He's lost a little weight, but not enough to be concerned," said the vet. "I have a new product which should help." She handed Caroline a packet about the size of a restaurant wet wipe. "Sprinkle a few of these little papers in his litter box. If he has too much sugar in his urine, they'll turn red."

"Too much sugar?" asked Caroline's mom. "But you just said his sugar was low. How do we test for that?"

"We can't really. You have to keep an eye on him. If he gets lethargic again, it probably means he's had too much insulin. You can put a bit of syrup on your finger and wipe it on his gums. It should revive him, and then get him in here as fast as you can, but most important: give him as much water as he wants. Dehydration is as dangerous as a coma."

"So, he's going to be all right?" asked Caroline. Her stomach was a tight knot that even Casey's gentle purr couldn't soothe.

"Well, I'm not going to lie," Dr. Kowalsky said, "I'd like to see his diabetes stabilized. I'm going to test his thyroid again. His levels were borderline high at his last exam. It may be time to medicate for that, too."

She stroked Casey's orange fur from head to tail. Caroline was thankful to have a doctor who so obviously cared about animals.

"His fur feels great, for an old guy. I can see you're taking good care of him."

Caroline smiled weakly at the compliment. She'd remember it next time Dad called Casey a spoiled rotten cat.

At home, Caroline forgot all about homework. She put ice in a bowl and filled it with water. Casey liked ice-water. She sat on the floor and rubbed his back while he drank. He rewarded her with a purr. Tears suffocated her when she thought about how close they had come to losing him.

"Time for bed," said her mother.

"I'll wait for him to finish," Caroline said, "then we'll both go to bed."

Mom only nodded. She had long ago given up the fight to keep Casey off the bed, and tonight Caroline needed him as much as he needed her.

Chapter Three

Caroline read her ecology chapter on the bus the next morning. If she could get her math homework done at lunch she might actually make it through the day without a scolding. She sat at the front of the bus, so her friends wouldn't disturb her.

"You don't have ignore your friends for me." Aimee looked over the bus seat at her. Caroline knew she was being sarcastic, but she wasn't in the mood for Aimee Jones' games.

"I'm not. My cat was sick last night and I didn't have time to do my homework."

"You have a cat? How come I've never seen him? I've got an old tomcat. I'm surprised they haven't been fighting like devils." Caroline made a mental note to keep Casey in at night. He wasn't strong enough to battle over territories with another cat.

"He doesn't wander too much anymore," she said. "He's old."

"Oh."

Caroline waited for Aimee to make some mean comment about putting old cats down, but she shrugged and went back to her book.

By the time they arrived at school, Caroline had read the same page of her textbook four times, and couldn't remember a word.

Let's hope old Besner is deaf, dumb and blind, Caroline thought as she headed to class completely unprepared. Maybe then she'd get through class without looking like an idiot.

"Come on, Caroline," Brenda nearly pulled her off the bus. "We're going to the convenience store before class starts."

"Can't," said Caroline. "I need to finish my homework before homeroom."

"Blow it off." Brenda grinned in that way she had when she really wanted something.

Caroline considered for a moment. It was only the first week of school. She could easily catch up.

"I'll go with you," Jimmy said, coming up behind them. Brenda's grin turned into a blush.

"Okay, see ya, Caroline."

They went off to join another group of kids waiting to go.

I guess I won't go. Caroline tried not to feel left out. Brenda had asked her after all, but she hadn't given her the chance to answer.

She looked at her watch. Twenty-five minutes until first bell. She found a quiet corner and tried again to read her ecology text.

"Give it back, Moron." Aimee's angry voice broke into her concentration. A boy dangled a purple notebook with "Aimee" scrolled all over it above the girl's head. Caroline knew the boy, but couldn't remember his name.

"You are so dead, Andrew!" Aimee yelled.

"What's in this book, anyway? Love poems? A diary. Let's see." Holding the book above Aimee's head, he reached up with his other hand to flip it open. Aimee slugged him in the gut. Andrew let out a loud "ooof," dropped the book and doubled over. By this time, a large crowd had gathered around. Aimee picked up her notebook and sat back on the bench as if nothing had happened.

"Freak," Andrew said before walking away with his friends. Punch in the stomach or not, Andrew wouldn't fight a girl, especially one who might beat him.

"Loser," Aimee said under her breath. Caroline wanted to say something, but what did you say to a friend who was not a friend, who'd been insulted then punched a boy? The more she hung around Aimee, the less she understood her. Of course, Aimee would say they didn't hang.

"How come you only hit boys?" Caroline asked as she sat on the bench.

"Because no girl has ever pissed me off enough, but you're working on it." She stood up and left the bench to Caroline and her ecology text.

Can you say repressed aggression?

The bell rang, and Caroline still hadn't read her homework.

⁓

Caroline took her old bus home and got off with Brenda. She'd been back to the neighborhood a few times since the move, but it was still weird to see someone else's car parked in her old driveway. The new owners had changed a few things. Her swing set was gone and they'd built a stone pathway leading to the front door.

"Don't they have kids?" Caroline asked.

"Nope," Brenda said. "Mom said they were only recently married."

Caroline had come home with Brenda to work on their English project. They were supposed to pick a song and analyze it in front of the whole class. Brenda hated speaking in front of people, so Caroline had agreed to do the presentation, but they hadn't yet picked a song, and the project was due the next day.

They cleared a work-space on Brenda's desk. Her room was disgusting. Crumpled clothes and plates of dried food covered everything. The desk was so sticky that Caroline held her binder on her lap. Brenda munched on a bag of chips she found under the chair and booted up her computer.

"I really think we should do 'My Love," she said.

Figures you would want to do a love song, thought Caroline. "That's so sappy," she said aloud. "I thought we could find something, you know, meaningful. Like 'Biko.'"

"What's 'Biko?'"

"Not what, who. He was an anti-apartheid activist." Caroline's parents were big Peter Gabriel fans. She'd grown up listening to his songs and her dad had told her all about Stephen Biko and his fight for justice.

"Anti-apartheid is so yesterday," Brenda said. "Love songs are eternal."

Caroline rolled her eyes. Luckily, her back was to Brenda and her friend didn't see.

"Okay," she said, "but I think we'll get more brownie points if we pick something that Mr. Klein recognizes."

"Oh, don't be such a suck up. Besides, I'm sure that Klein thought up this assignment to prove he's in tune with us. As if he ever could be."

Brenda was probably right. Klein would expect them to pick something from their own generation.

"Maybe, but let's find something better. Something to shock the pants off him."

Brenda smiled, and Caroline was glad to see they could still be on the same wave-length. They searched the media browser, jotting down a list of possible songs. Before they went any further, the doorbell rang.

"It's probably Jimmy." Brenda jumped up and ran downstairs to the door.

Jimmy. Oh no!

He lived one street away. Brenda and Caroline had played with him since they were five, if name-calling and trickery were a kind of play. Jimmy and his friend, Roger, had been their arch-enemies and the girls had sworn to hate them forever. They'd crashed the boy's snow forts and had their snowmen destroyed in return. During the summer, the battle for playground rights had been unending. Brenda and Caroline had once paid Jimmy's little brother to say their mother wanted him home, so the girls could have the park to themselves. Then they'd snuck into their secret fort inside the heavy thicket and planned more nefarious tricks.

The battle had fizzled out when they entered middle school. Jimmy and Roger were unimportant next to all the new friends they'd made. Suddenly it seemed childish to hate boys. They'd left ownership of the park to younger kids, and Brenda and Caroline began to ignore Jimmy and Roger on the bus.

As it should be. Caroline didn't understand how Brenda could be interested in Jimmy. They'd seen him wet his pants in the playground when he was six! It wasn't something you forgot.

But sometime since Caroline had moved out of the neighborhood, Brenda had stopped ignoring Jimmy. If Caroline hadn't left, would Brenda still hate Jimmy like she was supposed to?

"Hey, Caroline?" Brenda called up the stairs. "I'll be out back for a minute." She didn't wait for an answer.

Great. Left alone in Brenda's bedroom, Caroline continued to browse for a song. When Brenda didn't come back after ten minutes, she considered going downstairs to remind her about their homework.

She looked at her watch. Her mother wouldn't be here to pick her up for another hour. She could call, but she'd have to explain why she was coming home early, and she didn't want to admit to…to what? Was she jealous of Jimmy? A little, but mostly she was mad at Brenda for blowing her off.

She looked out the back window. Brenda and Jimmy were cuddling on a bench, almost hidden by the wisteria that climbed over the deck. Their heads were bent low as if they were whispering to each other. Caroline wondered if they were talking about her. No, that would be ridiculous. They were talking about nothing, the way new couples did. Caroline couldn't understand it. What was the point? Brenda laughed at something Jimmy said, but it wasn't Brenda's normal laugh. It was a fake, look-how-sophisticated-I-am laugh.

Caroline turned back to the computer, angry now. Brenda was such an airhead! And she was going to leave her to do the entire project. Fine.

She printed out the lyrics to Biko and began to interpret the words according to what her father had told her about his story. She checked the internet to fill in a few gaps. An hour later, she had a pretty decent presentation.

She looked out the window. Brenda was still flirting with Jimmy on the back deck.

She's practically sitting in his lap! Caroline thought, when she looked out the window again. She couldn't stand it any longer. She printed out two copies of their project and left one on Brenda's desk with "You're welcome!" scribbled across it in red pen, packed up her books and let herself out the front door without saying goodbye.

Her mother found her walking up the boulevard.

"What's the matter?" she asked as Caroline swung her bag into the car.

"Nothing. We finished early and I didn't feel like sticking around."

"Why not?"

"Jimmy was there."

"Oh." Mom was quiet for a few minutes concentrating on the traffic. "Maybe it's time to quit your feud with Jimmy and Roger. You're getting to that age where boys aren't supposed to be gross."

"Yeah, well I guess I'm a little slow." Caroline couldn't keep the bitterness from her voice. "Because Brenda sure figured that one out."

"What do you mean?"

"I mean she was practically sitting in his lap!"

"And that makes you mad?"

"No! Of course not. I'm mad because Brenda left me to do our entire homework project by myself, and tomorrow she'll get credit for it anyway."

"I see."

Caroline couldn't stand it when her mother said "I see" in that way, as if there was so much more to see than she let on. Well this time there wasn't. Brenda had blown her off and that was all.

"You know, honey, when you find a boy that interests you, you might understand Brenda's feelings better."

"I understand just fine."

"Well, then I guess you'd better talk to her about it."

"Whatever," Caroline said, and her mom let the subject drop.

Chapter Four

Brenda cornered Caroline as soon as she got off the bus the next morning. "So what's your problem, and why did you run off yesterday?"

"I didn't run off," Caroline said. "It was time to go home."

"Well, you didn't say goodbye."

"You were kinda busy, and I didn't want to intrude."

"As if." Brenda snorted. "Any way, I told you I didn't want to do Biko."

Caroline stared at her friend in amazement.

"I can't believe you!" she said. "I do our entire assignment while you're busy sucking face with Jimmy—and I can't tell you how much that grosses me out—and you don't like the song I picked."

"We weren't sucking face!" Brenda yelled. Heads turned their way. People were staring now. A fight between best friends was always entertaining. "And you'd better not tell anybody that we were."

"Why not?" Caroline sneered. "Are you ashamed of your new boyfriend?"

"He's not my boyfriend. He's…I don't know. But you have no right to go starting rumors."

"I have every right! You blew me off, and I did our whole assignment!"

"Like I asked you to. Anyway, you know nothing about it."

"About what?"

"Guys." Brenda dropped the word between them like a stone. "You know nothing about guys. You're so…immature."

Tears pushed against Caroline's eyes. By now, most of the student body had stopped to listen to their fight. She couldn't let them see her cry. Turning from Brenda, she walked as fast as she could to the girls' bathroom.

She stared at herself in the mirror. Her face was red and her eyes glassy with unshed tears. She splashed cold water on her face. She didn't have to worry about make-up. She didn't wear any. Another difference between her and Brenda.

When had these differences become so great they couldn't even get along? Brenda didn't care much for their friendship. She was probably out there right now, laughing at her with Cindy, Heather and

Andrea. They'd get a big kick about the way Brenda had suckered Caroline into doing their assignment all alone.

Well, she wouldn't get away with it.

Caroline dried her face and went to find her English teacher, Mr. Klein.

After she told him the story (minus the part about Brenda and Jimmy) Mr. Klein leaned back in his chair and stared at her for a few minutes. Caroline squirmed in her chair. He didn't look at all pleased, and somehow his anger was directed at her.

"Are you sure you want to accuse Brenda of shirking her duties?" he asked.

"Well, yeah. I mean, I did everything."

"Fine." He asked a passing student to find Brenda and tell her to see him. While they waited, Mr. Klein continued to grade assignments, leaving Caroline to her own thoughts—thoughts that didn't hold the conviction they'd had while she was in the bathroom. Now she wondered if she'd been mistaken to come to Mr. Klein. You never knew how teachers were going to react.

Brenda finally walked into the office and shot Caroline a "You're Dead" look.

"Caroline tells me she did the project by herself. Is this true, Brenda?"

"Well…"

For a minute, Caroline thought Brenda would deny it, and she got ready to protest. She could prove she'd done all the work. After all, what did Brenda know about Stephen Biko.

"No, I guess I didn't really help," Brenda said.

Good. Now she's going to get it.

"I see," Mr. Klein said. "You realize I should fail you on this project then."

Caroline didn't smile. This was what she'd wanted, but somehow it didn't feel as good as she'd expected.

"But I'll give you a chance. Caroline, you'll read your presentation today. Brenda, you have one more night to come up with your own."

Both the girls nodded and rose to leave.

"Ladies." Mr. Klein's stern voice stopped them. "I hope you realize that this assignment was about more than analyzing a song. It was about teamwork, too. I will take this into consideration when I grade both your presentations."

Brenda grinned, and Caroline's heart sank.

It wasn't fair!

Outside Mr. Klein's office, Brenda pushed her against the wall.

"Consider our friendship over, Caroline. Why don't you go home and play with your dolls?"

Caroline watched her best friend walk away and

couldn't help thinking their friendship had been over for some time.

⤸

She was unusually tired, and she surprised her parent when, at eight o'clock, she told them she was going to bed. She scooped up Casey with one arm and headed upstairs. Her feet dragged like lead. Her eyes ached as if she'd been reading too long. She put on her pajamas, brushed her teeth, and fell into bed.

Before turning off the light, she looked around her room as if seeing it for the first time. A collection of dolls from around the world was displayed on her dresser, but she didn't play with them. Brenda didn't understand the value of such a collection. Her room was always a mess. The only thing she collected was dirt.

Caroline glanced at her desk. Photos covered the bulletin board, most of them pictures of her and Brenda. At the beach when they were only two. All dressed up for their first day of school, plus a series of silly black and whites, taken in a booth at the mall. Caroline got out of bed and took them all down. She couldn't bring herself to rip them up, so put them away at the bottom of her desk drawer with all the other junk she didn't need to think about.

She turned off the light and snuggled under the covers. The nights were getting chilly. Casey walked up her leg, onto her hip and then her shoulder. He sat beside her, purring like a madman until she lifted the blankets for him.

"Okay, okay."

He tucked himself under the blankets against her chest. Her arms circled him as if he were a teddy bear. Caroline tried not to think of Brenda calling her a baby.

"I don't care what she thinks," she whispered to Casey. He answered her back with a deep, rumbling purr that soon put her to sleep.

In her dreams, she walked along a country road, edged by thick brambles. It was all so familiar, yet she'd never been there before. Casey called to her from the other side of the bushes, but every time she tried to push through, the branches moved to block her way. She ran up the endless road, looking for a break in the thicket. Casey's cries became desperate. She reached into her pocket, looking for a knife or anything to cut the branches, and pulled out the pink stone. Brandishing it like a weapon, she held it out, and the bushes parted to let her through. The stone beach spread out before her, impossibly pink and shining so brightly it hurt her eyes.

… And still Casey cried.…

Caroline rolled over in her bed, shaking the dreams from her sleep. Casey turned around twice and settled behind her knees.

Chapter Five

By late September, Caroline had figured out most of her teachers. Miss Besner was okay as long as Caroline did the reading. Mr. Klein hadn't held the fiasco with Brenda against her, and she was doing well in his class. All in all, Caroline had a handle on her classes, but the homework was piling up. It seemed to breed in her backpack. Every time she finished one assignment, there were two new ones to research. She needed a break.

"Mom, have you seen Casey?" Caroline yelled down the stairs to the laundry room where her mother folded clothes.

"He's out," Mom called back, "unless Dad let him in."

But Dad was in his office. He couldn't have let the cat in. Caroline looked in all Casey's favorite sleeping places: the spare room bed, the corner of the living room beside the heating vent, tucked under the table on one of the dining room chairs. She looked outside. He was nowhere.

Worry stewed in her stomach, but she held it back. She should go look for him now, but she had a lot of homework. Old Besner hadn't been impressed with her this morning. She had last night's chapter to read and tonight's. Plus a math quiz tomorrow.

She settled down at her desk to read. One good thing about their new house was her big bedroom with a small office attached. Here, she could do her homework in peace without her parents peering over her shoulder all the time. She resisted the urge to read in bed, because she was tired enough to fall asleep.

She finished the first chapter and half of the second before her mind wandered. The sun had lowered enough to shine right through her bedroom window and onto her desk. She looked up and let it warm her face. The feeling reminded her of the stone beach. When she closed her eyes, she could see the pink stones shining into the horizon. The image didn't seem like a memory, but more like an often repeated dream.

She was sorry she had to share the secret of the stone beach with Aimee Jones. Why did she have to be so mean? Caroline felt sure Aimee hid a kind person somewhere behind the rough face she put on at school. She'd seen it at the stone beach. She didn't care enough for the strange girl to find the agreeable person inside, and yet… and yet she felt obliged to seek her out. It was an uncomfortable burden.

She finished her homework as her mother called her down for dinner.

"Has Casey come in yet?" she asked. Her mother served only two plates. Dad was working late in his office.

"I haven't seen him," she said, then looked at Caroline's worried face and added, "I'm sure he's fine. Probably enjoying the last of the warm weather."

Caroline nodded, but she didn't believe her. Something was wrong. She could feel it. Mom would say her imagination was over active, so she kept the feeling to herself, but as she answered questions about school and her new classes, Caroline listened with only one ear. She trained the other on the back door, waiting for the telltale plucking sound of Casey's claws on the screen.

After supper, she told her mom she was going to study outside in the gazebo.

"That's great. I'm glad you're starting to enjoy the garden. But it's getting dark, so don't be long."

Caroline nodded and headed out into the back yard with her math book under one arm. She left it on the bench in the gazebo and took the path down to the river.

The sun was dark shades of pink and red. The magic light burnished the leaves gold and painted the garden in dream colors.

Caroline didn't bother to stop and take in the beauty. Her eyes fixed on the underbrush, looking for any sign of Casey. Down by the river, she called his name.

What if he'd slipped on a rock and fallen into the river? Would he be strong enough to pull himself out? What if some wild animal found him? Caroline had heard rumors that coyotes prowled these woods. One of her friends at school had found only her cat's little white paws.

Why had her parents moved them to this awful place?

"Casey! Casey!"

She felt foolish calling him, but she was far enough from the house that no one would hear her. She walked along the river's edge toward the stone beach and was so intent on peeking under every shrub, she didn't see the river open up before her until she came right up to the beach. When she saw the pink stones under her feet, she looked up and held her breath for a moment. The stones were a mirror of the sunset sky. The river was smooth obsidian, and the sun lit the willows from behind so they glowed like gold lace.

This is truly the most beautiful place on earth. She sat on a large rock to enjoy the play of light.

"I never should've shown you this place." Aimee clambered onto the rock beside Caroline. She carried the same purple book which had caused the fight earlier in the week.

"Now I guess I have to share it with you," she added.

Caroline said nothing. She wasn't in the mood for Aimee tonight. Casey was lost. It was getting dark, and she'd have to leave him outside to fall prey to whatever the night would bring.

They watched in silence for a while as the last light faded, leaving the stone beach in shadow. Suddenly, from high in the trees behind them, Caroline heard yelling. She tensed for a moment, thinking her mom had called, but no. The voices were an angry man and woman. They were too far away to hear the argument, but the rage was clear enough. Something shattered. The voices were quiet for a moment and then exploded again, louder than before.

"I guess I can't even escape them here," Aimee said. Caroline was about to ask who, when she noticed the strange expression on Aimee's face, embarrassment. She hadn't thought it possible to embarrass the brash Aimee Jones.

"My parents." Aimee shrugged as if it explained everything.

"Oh." Caroline hated herself for uttering such a stupid response. She didn't know what to say. Her parents rarely argued, and never with such outright rage. How did Aimee stand it?

The two girls sat on the stone beach, listening to the parent-storm above them. Caroline was too embarrassed to get up and leave now, as if it would make it worse somehow. Aimee, clearly, had nowhere else to go.

Eventually the storm blew itself out. Aimee still made no move to leave, despite the growing dark. Caroline's mother would worry about her, but she couldn't make herself leave. Not without saying something.

"So how come you spell your name that way?" she asked, pointing to the notebook with "Aimee" scrawled all over it.

"It's French. My grandma's from the south. They still speak French there, or something like it." She smiled at Caroline wryly. "It means 'loved'."

Caroline smiled back at her.

"That's pretty sucky," she said. Both of them seemed to know, Caroline would never tell another soul Aimee's name meant something so mushy.

"Yep," Aimee said. "I sure feel the love."

The girls burst into nervous laughter that turned genuine.

"I think my parents were hippies," said Aimee, catching her breath.

"Mine still are. If I have to hear one more time about the benefits of compost, I'm gonna puke."

After another moment of companionable quiet, Aimee asked, "So what are you doing out here, anyway?"

"Looking for my cat. I haven't seen him all day. I'm worried he might be hurt."

"You know," Aimee said, "cats often go off to hide when they're about to die. It's instinctual or something."

"Why do you always have to do that?" Caroline jumped to her feet.

"Do what?"

"You know what!" Caroline's voice cracked, and she fought back tears.

Not now. Not it front of Aimee.

"I don't know what you're talking about, Spaz. I was telling the truth."

"It might be true, but it's really mean."

"So sue me."

"See what I mean?" Caroline said. Anger had

won out over the tears. "Every time you're nice to me for even a minute, you have to ruin it. You're such a…such a…jerk!"

She spun to leave and her ankle turned on a stone. She went down with a thud, banging her knee and scraping both hands.

"Dammit!" she swore. Aimee always made her feel so awkward and small. There was nothing nice in her. No point looking for what wasn't there.

As Caroline got to her feet, Aimee shushed her.

"Shush yourself," Caroline said, but Aimee waved curtly with one hand while she listened to the night.

A pathetic mewling came out of the bush behind them, followed by a bedraggled cat.

"Casey!"

Caroline ran toward him, ignoring the pain in her leg. Then she noticed the strange way he walked, as if he were drunk. And his meow was almost strangled in his throat. He took another step and his back legs collapsed on him.

"Oh, Casey!"

She sat beside him and stroked him all over, looking for broken bones. He didn't hiss at her touch, so he wasn't in any pain. In fact, he purred. Caroline wondered if it was a nervous purr. He did that sometimes at the vet.

"I've got to get him home," she said. "Something's wrong."

"Wait!" Aimee stared into the bushes. The night was silent. Unnaturally silent. No crickets, no frogs, no rustling leaves. A chill shook Caroline. As she bent to pick Casey up, a shadow burst out of the bushes, knocking her to the ground.

Except she'd felt nothing, even as it pushed past her. No, not past her. Through her!

Another long wraith erupted from the bushes, and then another and another until the beach filled with the bounding shadows. They ran along the edge of the river, never touching the water.

"They're cats!" Caroline hissed.

Orange cats, black cats, striped, calico. Hundreds of cats.

She held onto Casey as the ghostly cats ran around them. He mewled, and Caroline bent herself over him, protecting him from the wraiths. They caterwauled with ear-splitting howls. Caroline covered her ears but nothing could block out the piercing noise. She shut her eyes tight, but she could still feel the wind against her skin as they swirled around her.

Casey squirmed in her arms, and Caroline held on tight. The ghost cats wanted him. Deep in her heart, she knew it. They wanted to drag him off on their monstrous hunt.

They screamed and raced around the beach until Caroline thought she would go mad.

Then, as suddenly as they'd appeared, they were gone. Caroline opened her eyes to see the last ones running on sleek soundless paws along the river's edge. They melted away, shadows into shadows.

In the silence that followed, Casey mewed. One of his eyes drooped shut. Caroline had to get him home, but she couldn't move. She looked over at Aimee, who also looked frozen in place. Aimee met her eyes and shook her head.

There was nothing to say.

Chapter Six

The clinic was closed, but Caroline's mother had called the emergency number and Dr. Kowolsky had agreed to meet them despite the late hour. The vet clinic was still deserted when they arrived.

"Stay in the car," Mom said. "I'll see if Dr. Kowalsky is here yet."

Caroline held Casey on her lap. He'd meowed the entire ride. It was a miserable attempt at a yowl, like a squeaky toy losing its air. Over and over, he tried to lift one paw as if he didn't know what it was for. His eye drooped and his third eyelid covered it halfway.

"The door's locked," her mother said, getting back in the car. They waited in silence. Mom had already scolded her for being down by the river after dark. It seemed so unimportant now, such a small transgression since it meant she'd found Casey.

Caroline was sorry she hadn't found him in time. Those phantom cats had done this to him. She was certain. How long had they been chasing him before he found her?

"Mom," Caroline said, "I saw something. By the river. I mean, Aimee saw it too."

"Saw what?"

Caroline didn't know where to begin. How did you tell a grownup, monsters really did live in the shadows, without sounding like a scared kid?

Except that she was a kid. And she was scared. She needed help.

"I don't know what they were. Cats, I guess. Lot's of them."

Another car pulled into the parking lot and Dr. Kowolsky got out. She motioned for them to follow her into the clinic. By the time Caroline wrapped Casey in his blanket and made it inside, the vet had turned on all the lights.

"Bring him here," the doctor said, pointing to the steel examining table.

Casey tried to get off the table, but each time he rose on wobbly legs, he managed only a step before falling. Dr. Kowolsky took his temperature and looked into his eyes. She felt him all over for broken bones or cuts.

"Caroline said there were other cats," Mom said.

"Has he been fighting? Could a cat fight hurt him this bad?"

"I don't think so," said the doctor. "I don't feel any sort of trauma. But of course, cat's claws are so sharp, he may have puncture wounds I can't find. We'll only know if they abscess in a few days." She continued to examine him for several more minutes.

Caroline bit her lip, trying not to get angry. Casey was pitiful. Those horrible creatures had been chasing him when he could barely walk.

Dr. Kowolsky put her stethoscope down. Casey tried to stand again, and she gently held him down with one hand, smoothing his prickly fur.

"I'm afraid Casey's had a stroke," she said.

"A stroke?" Caroline knew what it was, but only vaguely.

"But wouldn't it have, you know, killed him?" her mother asked. She was obviously uncomfortable talking about this in front of Caroline, but knew better than to ask her daughter to wait outside.

"Not necessarily," said the doctor. "Casey's a real trooper." She smiled at Caroline as if this was her doing. "And it might have been a minor stroke."

Caroline felt as if the room spun around her in ever tightening circles. "Please, what is a stroke?"

"It's a blood clot in the brain," said the doctor. "The clot blocks oxygen and that kills brain cells.

Which functions were affected will depend on where the clot is."

"Brain cells?" asked Caroline. "That's why he's walking funny?"

"Yes. He's lost some motor skills."

"But they will come back. Right?"

"I don't know, Caroline." Dr. Kolowsky's face and voice took on the tender quality someone gets, right before they give bad news. "It will depend on you and Casey. But I think you have to start preparing yourself. The kindest thing might be to put him down."

"No!" Caroline's mind howled like a cat in pain.

"They did this to him," she said, "those other cats." She needed someone to blame, to take her thoughts away from the idea of Casey dying.

"No, I don't think so," said the vet. "A stroke is not brought on by over exertion like a heart attack. It's more likely his diabetes is the cause."

"Are you sure it's a stroke?" her mother asked. "Could it be an infection?"

"Yes, and I'll run some blood tests to be sure, but in the mean time, we should start treating him for a stroke immediately. The first few hours after the stroke are the most important for a good chance of recovery. He'll need constant care. He's confused and scared. He may need help getting into his litter box and to his food bowl."

"I'll have to cancel my appointments tomorrow," Mom said.

"No, Mom. I want to take care of him."

"You have school."

"I'll miss a day. It's Friday and that'll give me three whole days to be with him. To help him. It's no big deal."

"It is a big deal, Caroline. School is more important…" She almost said, more important than a cat, but stopped when she saw Caroline's expression. "All right. You can stay home one day."

"That's good," Dr. Kowolsky said . "You're the reason Casey is still fighting to be alive. I'm sure you can do a lot to help him." She took Caroline's hand and laid it on Casey's back. She could feel the gentle rumble of his purr. "But you can't expect him to get better in three days. This will take a long time and he may never be altogether like you remember him."

Caroline nodded. Tears blurred her eyes, but she tried not to cry. Animals could sense things like sadness, and she wanted Casey to feel only her love.

The vet took some blood and explained his new medication. Caroline wrapped Casey back in his blanket and took him home.

CHAPTER SEVEN

The next day was the hardest of her life. Her mother left early in the morning.

"I'll be in my office, intercom me if you need anything," Dad said and stopped at the door, so Caroline nodded.

"And sweetie, I'm really proud of you for taking such good care of your friend."

Caroline smiled. If he knew what a mess she'd made of her other friends, he wouldn't be so quick to praise. But she didn't need to think of Brenda and her new boyfriend or the infuriating Aimee Jones. Casey needed her.

She'd never lost a loved one before. Not an uncle or aunt, and her grandparents had all passed away before she was born. Casey was the only pet she'd ever had. The idea of losing him terrified her, and brought up all kinds of questions she didn't want to think about. Where would he go? Was there a cat heaven? Was there a heaven at all?

She laid her head beside him and breathed in his warm smell. One day soon, he would be rotting in the ground.

She shivered away those thoughts and stood.

"Come on now. Let's get you something to eat."

She put a bowl of food on the floor beside his plush bed. He struggled to stand, but he couldn't get his feet to work in unison and landed heavily on his chin.

Caroline fought back tears. It was horrifying to see him so weak.

"It's okay, buddy. Come on, I'll help you."

Doctor Kowolsky had warned her against babying him too much.

"He won't learn to walk again if you carry him everywhere," she'd said.

So Caroline fought the urge to sweep him up in her arms and urged him to reach the food himself. Watching him, she became angrier and angrier. He was so frail, and yesterday he'd been so strong. Dr. Kowolsky had said the stroke hadn't been caused by the other cats, but Caroline wasn't so sure. After all, she'd not told the doctor everything.

Like the fact the cats had been ghosts.

Caroline sighed. Could she have dreamed it all?

She spent the rest of the morning talking to Casey, urging him to eat, to use his litter box or to move around. When she felt she'd pushed him as far as he could go, she lay down beside his bed and talked about their old house and his favorite hiding places. She sang to him and stroked his back while he slept.

Later she fed him wet food on the tips of her fingers and didn't even care about the horrible cat food smell. She cleaned up after him when, after struggling to get into his box, his bladder had released all over the floor. After that, she put away the box and found some old towels to take its place. She sprinkled some of his litter on the towel so he would know the smell.

She gave him water, helped him stand, encouraged him to walk and loved him as best as she could.

After a while, she decided it was best to let him rest. She opened her ecology text hoping to catch up on her missed chapters, but she couldn't concentrate on the qualities of tundra. She closed her book and booted up her computer.

She Googled "ghost cat" and read a few of the pages that popped up.

"...I swear I heard the pitter patter of little feet and then I felt something jump on my bed, but when I turned on the light nothing was there."

Or:

"I heard howling like a cat in heat outside my window. But I live on the third floor!"

The entries became even more ridiculous from there on. The people writing them sounded defensive and pushy. Between the lines Caroline could hear them say, "I don't care if you believe me or not, I saw it!" Caroline didn't know what to believe. Wouldn't she sound the same way if she tried to explain what she'd seen to someone else?

In any case, she didn't find any reference to a ghostly cat hunt. Domestic cats didn't run in packs, like lions or wolves. They were usually solitary creatures.

Caroline closed her eyes and let the memories she'd been avoiding rush into her head. There'd been so many! They'd overwhelmed her senses with their screeching and running about and yet…

And yet, they hadn't touched her. Or Aimee. Or Casey. But she couldn't get the idea out of her head that they'd wanted Casey. She was sure they'd been calling to him. Showing off their speed and voices, as if to entice him out of her arms.

Except, of course, the ghost cats didn't know Casey couldn't walk. Or maybe they did. Maybe they'd come to him because he was weak prey.

Or maybe they'd come to take him away, like angels of death.

They certainly hadn't looked like angels, but it made about as much sense as any other theory. She sighed and shut off her computer. She needed someone to talk to about this, but no one would believe her. She didn't trust Brenda to listen, not that Brenda would tear herself away from Jimmy long enough to listen. Only Aimee would understand, but she'd made it clear, because they'd crossed paths once in a while, they were anything but friends.

There was no one else.

No one but Casey. She'd depended on him for so long. He alone had listened to all her dreams, and fears. When she was little, her parents would send her to her room as punishment for temper tantrums, or not eating dinner, or any of the other thousand things that insulted parents. In her room, she used to whisper all her anger to Casey. Quietly, she'd rage at the unfairness of her parents and the world in general. Casey had listened with his eyes half closed, his fox tail swishing. And somehow, Caroline always felt better, as if Casey took away her anger, swished it away with a sweep of his tail.

She was, of course, too old to be sent to her room, but Casey still comforted her in a way that no one else could. He'd spent last night on his plush bed on the floor, and her bed had felt strangely cold and empty without him. She knew he was too weak to sleep on the bed. He wouldn't be able to get off if he needed to use the litter, and worse, he could even fall.

But she missed him already. It was a taste of what life would be like without him.

She gathered him up in her arms and brought him onto the bed for a snuggle. She was rewarded with a low steady purr and one pathetic flick of his tail. She kissed him on his nose, knowing he hated it, and stroked him from head to tail, because he loved it. She lay down with her cheek pressed against his side so she could feel the vibrations of his purr.

She barely noticed when the tears started streaming down her face. Not until her chest heaved with the effort of crying, and then she let it all out.

Finally.

Chapter Eight

School set into its predictable pattern, except Caroline found herself outside her clique of friends, looking in. She didn't really care. Brenda, Cindy, Heather and Andrea were strangers to her now. Every day, their clothes became more and more outrageous. Brenda had pierced her nose, and Caroline had a private laugh. Brenda's Mom must have had a fit when she saw it.

Brenda held hands with Jimmy as they walked down the halls. She leaned against him while they sat beside their lockers. She sat on his lap on the grass at recess.

And then, one day Caroline saw her walking hand in hand with Marco. Jimmy was no where to be seen. The next week it was Kevin.

Caroline was embarrassed for Brenda, because everyone began to talk about her. She was glad they were no longer friends, so it wasn't her job to tell Brenda she had a bad reputation. She wondered, did Cindy talk to her about it, or were they all afraid that Brenda would dump them as she'd dumped Caroline?

Brenda wasn't the only one with a boyfriend. It seemed as if the whole school had paired up. Cindy walked with Bill, and Andrea with Cliff. Even Aimee seemed very close to one of the punk heads, Karl. He was older, because he'd been held back a grade. He only wore black with heavy boots and black gloves with the fingers cut off.

Ever since the strange night at the stone beach, Aimee had become more friendly and didn't curse Caroline with every breath. They sat together on the bus and had even worked on a history project together. Caroline was surprised to find Aimee was really smart.

Without her old circle of friends, Caroline still felt lost in the sea of students at school. She was lonely, but would never admit it to anyone.

One lunch hour, she found herself at the same table as Jimmy. He watched Brenda sit down at a table across the hall with Kevin, and it was a long moment before Jimmy took his eyes off them.

Caroline felt sorry for him. After all, they'd been friends since kindergarten, even if they'd rarely spoken. Forgetting the old pictures of him in her head (Jimmy running through the sprinkler in his underwear or crying over a split knee), she had to admit he was kind of cute. He wasn't a little boy anymore, though his blond hair and blue eyes made him seem sweet.

"I'm sorry about you and Brenda," Caroline said.

Jimmy looked up from his lunch. "Yeah. It was pretty harsh."

Caroline wanted to say Brenda would come to her senses and go back to him, but they both knew it wasn't true. Brenda had discovered her power over boys, and Jimmy had only been her first conquest.

"You going to the dance next week?" She asked to make conversation, but as soon as the words left her mouth, she realized it sounded like a proposal.

"Nah," Jimmy said. "Well maybe. You?"

"I hadn't really thought of it. You want to go together?" She couldn't believe she'd asked him!

"Sure." He smiled at her, and her stomach fluttered, not unlike the fear she'd felt when she was over-run by the ghost cats.

Suddenly she wished she did wear makeup.

There was nothing left to say, so they sat in silence in the middle of the noisy cafeteria. Caroline hoped by the time the dance came around, one of them would have found something to talk about.

The afternoon passed like a dream. Caroline went to class and took notes, but she heard nothing. Between classes, she searched the halls for a glimpse of Jimmy, and when she did see him, turned and walked in the other direction, bumping into Aimee.

"I hear that Jimmy asked you to the dance," she said.

Caroline felt herself blush.

"Actually, I…uh, asked him."

"You go girl!" Aimee laughed. "There might be some hope for you yet."

Caroline smiled. Aimee's barbed compliments no longer bothered her.

"How's Casey?" Aimee asked.

"The same. He's walking better but won't eat much."

"That's some good news. Here." She handed her a printout entitled, *Animal Wraiths and Shades*. "I found this on the internet. It might interest you."

Caroline glanced at it. More silly sightings of would-be ghosts, told second or third hand. She sighed.

"We should go back to the beach and look for those cats." This was the second time Aimee had urged her to go back to the beach. Caroline didn't want to face those wraiths again, not even if Casey was safe inside.

"I told you I wasn't interested in finding them again."

"What, are you afraid?"

"Of course I'm afraid, and you should be too. Those…those things wanted something and I'm not sure it's a good idea to find out what."

Aimee didn't say anything else about it as they walked to class. They sat in their seats and pretended to listen to the teacher list the important dates in the Civil War. Aimee scribbled on a piece of loose-leaf. Caroline assumed it was another of her fantastic drawings. Her purple book was filled with her pen and ink drawings of fantasy creatures. She was good enough to draw her own graphic novel.

When the teacher's back was turned, Aimee leaned across the aisle and gave her the paper. It was a drawing of black cats, running in a blur across a rocky river. Their eyes shone with white light. The caption read, "Life's Little Mysteries Revealed."

Aimee was right. They'd had an opportunity to witness something unique. Something truly mysterious in a world of cold science. They should try to find the cats again. And yet, Caroline couldn't shake her fear. Those cats wouldn't divulge their mystery without a price.

She tucked the drawing under her text. Aimee had never given her one of her drawings before. She would keep this one.

Chapter Nine

Caroline was glad the dance wasn't formal. She was nervous enough without having to fuss with a fancy dress. As it was, she couldn't find a thing to wear, and her mother agreed to take her to the mall the afternoon of the dance to find an outfit.

Caroline wanted a blank tank dress, but her mother said no. After exhausting all the shops and compromising on a skirt and blouse, they ate ice cream at the food court.

"So, I assume you have a date for this dance," Mom said.

"Why do you say that?" asked Caroline.

"Because you've never worried about your clothes before."

Caroline smiled and looked down at her ice cream. She'd never talked to her mother about boys before, but found once she'd started, the words came easily.

"I'm going with Jimmy Douglas. He's going to meet me there."

"I thought he was Brenda's boyfriend."

"Yeah, well, she moved on, and on and on and on."

"Oh. Is that why you two are no longer friends?"

"I guess so. I mean I'm not really so sure. It's almost like Brenda outgrew me." Caroline tried not to let her mother see the tears prickling in her eyes. Why did she always have to cry?

"Actually," Mom said. "I've always felt Brenda wore two faces. If you're finally able to see past it, then maybe you're the one growing up and leaving Brenda behind."

Caroline hadn't thought of it that way. Brenda's recent behavior did seem like a spoiled child craving attention.

"Let's get going,"Mom said. "If we hurry, I can help you with your makeup."

Caroline smiled. "That'd be great."

∽

Dressed and made up, Caroline stood by the door to the school gym waiting for Jimmy. Nerves almost overtook her.

What if Jimmy had changed his mind? What if

he'd only said yes so he could stand her up and make her look a fool? What if…

Then she saw him. He wore jeans and a button down shirt open to reveal a black shirt underneath. Caroline couldn't even picture him as a little boy anymore.

"You look great," he said, taking her by the arm. Caroline resisted the urge to babble about her mother and shopping and makeup.

"Thanks," she said. "You too."

As they walked into the gym, she felt like everyone watched them, and the thought didn't terrify her.

The dance was slow going. Most people hadn't arrived yet and the gymnasium was nearly empty. No one wanted to be the first out on the floor. Jimmy and Caroline sipped sodas in a corner. Soon they were joined by Roger and his date, as well as some of his other friends. Caroline realized how much she'd missed this simple act of hanging around with friends. She also wondered why she'd let Brenda disturb her so much that she'd lost this. Their fight seemed so far away now.

Aimee joined them with her black-clad boyfriend. They were out of place in this crowd, but Aimee didn't seem to care. To Caroline's surprise, her boyfriend, Jason, knew Jimmy and Roger from lacrosse. *If Aimee can fit in here,* she thought, *then so can I.*

And Jimmy made it easy for her. He was no longer the little boy who'd stolen their Barbie's and wrecked their snowmen. Somewhere in the past few years, he'd grown up and she hadn't even noticed.

She noticed now.

He was funny and kind. He made sure she didn't feel left out, even though these weren't really her friends. He talked to her about his least favorite classes, making her laugh at his impression of Mr. Peterson.

Caroline felt herself lean into him, and he didn't pull away. She told him things she'd not even realized she was thinking. About going to high school in another year and how she felt pushed into choosing a profession too soon.

"I'm only fourteen, but already they want me to decide between sciences and language arts. I don't like either of them, really."

"I know what you mean," he said. "My parents want me to take all the advanced science courses so I'll be ahead, but the homework is killing me."

They talked about everything. She told him about Casey and his stroke. He was really interested in how she'd helped him rehabilitate. He remembered Casey from when they were kids. She didn't, of course, tell him about the ghost cats, though she could see Aimee watching and listening.

Aimee smiled her smirking smile, as if daring Caroline to tell. Caroline shot her a glance that said "lay off!"

Then someone started to cheer. The first couple had braved the dance floor.

Brenda and her newest guy from a neighboring school.

"Looks like she's already been through all the guys at this school," Roger said. Someone laughed nervously and a few people glanced at Jimmy to see how he'd react. Jimmy turned his back to the dance floor and continued his conversation with Caroline.

After a few minutes, more couples drifted onto the dance floor, and Jimmy held out his arm for Caroline to join him.

She'd been to dances before, but never with a date, so found herself concentrating solely on Jimmy. The other dancers faded into the flashing lights and blaring music. Neither of them could speak over the noise, but it only enhanced their sense of isolation.

They were the only two in the room.

When a slow song came on, Jimmy didn't head off the floor. He pulled Caroline close. His hand found the small hollow of her back. She tucked her head under his chin and breathed in his smell. Her hand could feel the thumping in his chest. They were both a little sweaty. They danced through one song then another.

Finally, as the last chords of the song ended, Jimmy pulled away. When Caroline looked up at him, he kissed her gently. The shock of it reached her toes, but Caroline didn't move until his lips left hers.

She held her breath, looking up at him. He seemed as stunned as she was. Then he smiled and took her by the hand, back to the safe circle of their friends.

Several dances later, Caroline went with Aimee to the girls' bathroom to freshen up. Their faces were damp and Caroline's makeup was smudged. She took out her compact and tried to fix it as best she could.

Someone bumped her hard against the porcelain sink.

Brenda.

"Don't you look cute," she said. "All dressed up like a big girl."

"At least I'm not dressed like a whore," Caroline said, and wondered when Brenda had grown so tall because she could barely see past her.

"Jimmy never minded the way I dressed."

"Yeah, well I guess he minded the way you latched on to any guy that walked by."

Brenda shoved her again. Caroline's hip banged up against the sink hard enough to bruise, but she wasn't going to let Brenda see her pain.

"You'd better watch your mouth, Caroline. You were always such a cry-baby. It shouldn't be too hard to make you cry now. I'd have no problem beating you until you bleed."

"I'd have a problem with that," Aimee said as she stepped out of the bathroom stall. Dressed in Goth style, with combat boots and multiple nose piercings, Aimee was intimidating at the best of times. Her scowl added to the dark aura. Brenda looked from Caroline to Aimee and back again. Caroline knew what she was thinking. Aimee was crazy. No one messed with her. She felt a new courage growing inside her.

"Jimmy doesn't even think of you anymore, Brenda. He's here with me."

"Yeah, you always wore my hand-me-downs."

Caroline bit her tongue so as not to scream the curses she was thinking. Brenda smirked again, and pushed past her.

How could I have ever been friends with her? Has she always been this mean?

Caroline knew the answer to that last question without really thinking: Yes. Brenda had always been the one to think up nasty tricks to play on others.

She'd made up all the mean names for the unpopular kids in elementary school, and started bad rumors about people she didn't like.

Brenda always had a mean streak. Only it had never been directed at Caroline before.

"Forget about her," Aimee said. "She's a cow."

Caroline smiled.

"I heard that Jimmy broke up with her anyway," Aimee said.

"Yeah, because he saw her kissing Marco. He still likes her I can tell."

"After tonight, all bets are off in that department."

Caroline smiled and the two girls—one dressed in a skirt and blouse, the other in black jeans and studded leather jacket—headed back to the dance.

Chapter Ten

"You sure it's all right with your parents that I take you home?" Jimmy asked. "I don't want to get you into trouble."

"When my mom heard it was little Jimmy Douglas taking me home, she knew nothing bad could happen," Caroline teased.

"Well, let's keep her thinking I'm only eight years old for a while longer, okay?"

He leaned over his scooter and kissed her briefly. It was enough to set her nerves on fire again.

Jimmy and Jason had their licenses to drive scooters. Jason said it was the closest he could get to a real motorcycle for another year. Jimmy gave Caroline his extra helmet. She climbed on the back of the bike and wrapped her arms around Jimmy's waist as they took off out of the parking lot. Caroline was amazed at how fast the scooter went. It was like a carnival ride. She yelled out like a battle call, and Jimmy drove faster down the country lane toward her house.

Aimee and Jason turned into her driveway, and Jimmy and Caroline continued on to hers. They'd left the dance early and Caroline still had some time before curfew. She took Jimmy's hand and led him around the back of the house, past her father's barn. She decided to finally put that gazebo to some good use. The lights from the house were enough to brighten their faces. Jimmy sat on the gazebo's bench and pulled Caroline down beside him. She expected him to kiss her again and turned her face up towards his. Instead, he took her hands.

"I'm sorry for what Brenda did to you in the bathroom," he said.

"Oh, you heard about that."

"It's a small school. Everyone heard about it. What I heard though, is that you stood up to her. Brenda's a bully, she always was. I'm glad you told her off."

Caroline laughed. "It's easy to be brave when Aimee Jones has your back."

"Yeah, she is a little crazy." He smiled at her. "But seriously. I'm really proud of you."

Caroline felt herself blush in the darkness, and then Jimmy did kiss her and she forgot everything else except for the feel of his hand in her hair.

He pulled away from her before she had the chance to worry if he would take it too far.

"I really like you, Caroline. I always did."

"Right, like I was really hot when I played with Barbie's and made mud pies."

"I'm not kidding," said Jimmy. "I don't want to mess this up."

Caroline nodded, not trusting her voice. Could it be true? Jimmy had always liked her in secret? It was a ridiculous thought, something which happened to other girls.

"Besides you looked so cute in that pink frilly bikini…You were what five? Six? Hot! Hot! Hot!"

"You jerk." She laughed and punched him on the shoulder. Her memories of Jimmy as a little boy no longer seemed like a hindrance. They were a comfort during this strange journey of discovering guys and worse, discovering herself in the eyes of a guy.

"Yeah, well you were pretty hot in your bathing suit too," she said. "It hung down to your ankles…"

"Shush!" he said, twisting in his seat to look out into the dark forest behind the gazebo.

"What?"

"I thought I heard something. There! Did you hear it?"

Caroline strained her ears and then she heard it too. A mewling sound like a hurt kitten.

"Casey!"

She jumped up and ran out of the gazebo. Jimmy followed behind her. He didn't need to be told that Casey shouldn't be out by himself in the dark.

Caroline stumbled through the dark bushes. She couldn't see the pathway, but she knew it took them down to the river. She stopped, listened again and there it was, the pained meow of a frightened cat.

She picked up the pace, down to the river and along the shore, right to the stone beach. There was no time to admire the moonlit beauty.

Casey lay in a crumpled heap on the stones. His back legs dragged in the water.

Caroline rushed over and gathered him up. He was soaked. He didn't even try to move, but hung limply in her arms.

"Oh no!" the sound ripped from her throat already tight with tears. "Oh, no." She rocked him back and forth. Jimmy didn't interrupt. This was her moment alone with her friend.

And then, the caterwauling began. The cats appeared from every shadow. Instinctively, Caroline bent low over Casey, sheltering him, as Jimmy wrapped his arms around Caroline. The cats swelled over them like a wave. Their cries were deafening. The sound brought fear and nausea. The wraiths circled them mercilessly, screeching their need.

They wanted Casey. Caroline hung on to him,

even as the creatures battered at her with their insubstantial bodies.

"No!" she yelled, but her voice was only a whisper in the noise of their screaming. "You can't have him!"

Even as she yelled these words, Casey got his second wind and struggled from her grip. She tried to hang onto him, but he had the strength of the desperate.

"Caroline, let him go." Jimmy's voice was only a whisper in her ear, though he shouted.

"No!"

"You're hurting him!"

Caroline looked down. He fought against her grip. Horrified, she let him go. He flopped on the stone beach like a fish out of water. The ghost cats ceased their wailing and stood silently, like an army watching and waiting.

Casey struggled to stand. It broke Caroline's heart to see him so weak, but she understood now it was his struggle. On his feet, he faced the army of wraiths. They were unmoved and unmoving.

Caroline reached out a tentative hand and stroked Casey's wet fur. He purred and leaned into her caress.

"My boy," she whispered. "My best boy."

He turned, with his new-found strength, and butted her with his head.

"I get it now," she said. Tears flowed freely down her face and she was unashamed.

"Go with them, old boy. I get it."

With that, Casey turned and struggled over the slippery stones toward the waiting wraiths. They took him into their fold and their strength boosted him. He stood suddenly upright, no longer a bedraggled old cat, but the picture of a fine young feline. The picture Caroline had always kept of him in her head.

"Go," she whispered.

And he did.

The cats took off into the shadows like the wing of one giant crow, leaving the feeble humans alone on the beach.

Caroline wept, hunched over the bare spot on the ground where Casey had been. Jimmy turned her towards him and held her in his arms until the sobs subsided.

When Caroline finally looked up through her blurry eyes, Aimee and Jason had joined them.

Aimee had no sarcastic remark, and Caroline was grateful. Instead, the four teenagers sat in silence, paying homage to a power they didn't understand and would never witness again.

Each of them felt proud to have been part of it that night.

Chapter Eleven

The Saturday after the dance dawned bright and warm, one of those perfect October days that defy the coming winter.

Caroline slipped out of the house before her parents woke. As she passed the gazebo, she paused to imagine herself sitting there with Jimmy. It all seemed so long ago, the dance, the kiss. She'd been a different person then. What they'd witnessed last night had changed her. She looked around at the sun lighting up the red and brown leaves. She listened to the rustle of squirrels, busy packing away their winter fare.

The woods were different today, more important now she knew other things lived out there too, things that no one else would believe. She liked that difference. It turned the farm she'd once hated into something special. It instilled in her the drive to learn something new every day, an impossible task certainly, but Caroline knew the effort wouldn't be wasted.

The only thing missing to make this a perfect day was Casey.

She headed down the wooded path to the river. The water was too cold to wade in, so she clambered over the rocks on the shore until she reached the stone beach.

It was even more beautiful today. The fall leaves added more color. Along with the shining pink stones, her senses were almost overloaded. Caroline shaded her eyes against the rising sun, and she saw him.

A little orange body lay crumpled on the rocks.

She stood frozen to the spot, wanting to go to him, but her legs knew better and wouldn't take her there. She sat heavily on a boulder.

I have to go to him. I should bury him.

What did it mean? She'd seen him run off with the ghost cats. Had it been a dream? If she asked Aimee or Jimmy about it, would they think she was crazy?

Aimee burst through the bushes carrying a shovel and stopped when she saw Caroline.

"I was down here earlier," she said. "I thought I would bury him so you wouldn't have to."

Caroline looked up at her friend. Fresh tears streaked her cheeks.

"I thought he wanted to go. What have I done?"

"No," Aimee said. "You did the right thing. He was supposed to go with them."

"Then why did they dump him there, like some bit of trash."

"Don't you get it? That's not Casey. They took the best part of him and left the shell."

Caroline was silent, unsure if she should let Aimee convince her.

"Listen, I've been thinking about this a lot since last night. Casey not only wanted to go with those cats, he had to. His body was no longer strong enough to hold his spirit. Those ghost cats came to show him the way."

"The way to where?"

"Well, that's the kicker, isn't it? We'll never know. We can only believe that it was to a good place."

Caroline wiped her face. Aimee was right. She had to believe. The alternative was madness. Besides, she owed it to Casey to believe that he knew what he was doing when he'd left her.

This opened up a whole knew set of questions, but Caroline was suddenly too tired to contemplate them. Besides, she had her whole life ahead of her to ponder such mysteries.

Aimee held out her hand and pulled Caroline to her feet. They dug a hole in the sand and buried Casey. Over his grave they piled bright pink stones.

As Caroline turned for home, she looked back and saw the pink monument shining in the morning sun like a beacon.

Epilogue

Casey padded through the dew-damp grass. His feet made no sound, even when he stepped on a fallen leaf. The dew didn't cling to his fur, nor did the scents of earth and fall rot tickle his nose.

Casey was no longer of this world. He knew that because his joints no longer ached, and he wasn't even tired. He felt young and strong again. But he'd stayed here too long. The Hunt called to him. He glanced into the trees where feline forms, now visible to him, flitted between the morning shadows. These were the spirits of cats who'd come before him, and he longed to run free with them. He had only one job to do before he could go.

He ran along the edge of the river where it wound around a bend, then followed the path to his family's house. To his Caroline.

She sat alone in the gazebo. The morning sun

lit her hair and streaks of tears on her cheeks. Casey wanted to run to her and nudge her hand with his nose. She'd stroke his fur from head to tail, and it would calm her. He could always sense it in the way her pulse slowed and her fingers relaxed. That was his job—to comfort Caroline.

But he couldn't do that anymore. He could only watch, his tail twitching restlessly.

Two figures came into the yard. A boy and a girl. He'd seen them with Caroline before. The boy put an arm around Caroline and she hugged him. The girl said something, and Caroline punched her in the arm, but it was a friendly gesture. They *were* friends.

Caroline laughed and wiped her tears. Friends were a good thing. He could leave her now, knowing she wouldn't be alone.

Casey's ears twitched. The Hunt called to him. He turned from his human family and ran to join the spirits of his heart.

Dear Reader,

What did you think of Caroline and Casey's journey? Some folks have told me they thought this was a sad story. I find it a joyful story. Caroline might have lost her two best friends, but she gained something more important—confidence. And Casey will never truly be gone from her heart. I'd like to think that his spirit is alive and running free with the Wild Hunt.

People often ask authors where they get their ideas for stories. This one comes from the heart. Casey was a real live cat who live with me through my college years, came with me when I married, and met my daughter when she was born. The only thing brighter than his orange fur was his pink nose. He was sixteen years old when diabetes finally took him from us. This story sparked in me one morning when my daughter (then only seven) asked, "What if Casey just doesn't wake up one morning?" I knew that was a possibility, but I suddenly realized how hard it was to talk about the death of a beloved pet. I'd lost a few as a child too, and I still had no words for my daughter. So I took a deep breath and said, "We'll just have to love him as best we can every day until that happens." And we did.

If you enjoyed Casey's story, I would appreciate it if you left a review at your favorite book store.

Reviews are important to every author, because they help other readers know what to expect from the book; they let me know how my books are received by readers; and they help booksellers decide which books to show to new readers. To leave your review for *The Stone Beach*, visit KimChatel.com/stone-beach-review.

And don't forget to sign up for my reading group. You'll get news about new releases and a free eBook just for signing up. Check it out at https://BookHip.com/QXRXNCM.

Thank you,

Kim Chatel

Mini-Moi is only six hands tall. He wants to work in the farm like the big horses, but he's too small. When Mini-Moi runs away, he finds a whole menagerie of animals in need. Children will delight in the animal antics as Mini-Moi discovers that even little ones can be big helpers. Learn French vocabulary and phrases along the way. Includes a glossary of French terms included in the story. Suggested reading age 5-9.

About the Author

 Kim Chatel is an author, fiber artist and photographer. She uses her art and books to inspire students to create their own. She can often be found at craft fairs near her home in Ontario, Canada with her books and a horde of needle-felted creatures. Kim writes adult fantasy fiction under her maiden name, Kim McDougall.

Visit Kim Chatel at www.KimChatel.com.

www.ingramcontent.com/pod-product-compliance
Lightning Source LLC
Chambersburg PA
CBHW050156110726